Princess
Baby

karen katz

schwartz & wade books • new york

Why doesn't anyone ever call
me by my REAL name?

It's always Good morning, Buttercup,
Time for breakfast, Giggly Goose,

Don't forget to brush your teeth, Cupcake,

Put your sweater on, Little Lamb, or
How's my Sweet Gumdrop today?

But I am not a buttercup

 or a giggly goose.

I am not a cupcake.

Please don't call
me Little Lamb,

and never *ever*
Sweet Gumdrop.

Please call me
by my real name.

You'll know me by my shiny crown,

my fancy dress,

my sparkly shoes,

my velvet cape,

my glittery jewels,

and, of course,
my royal wand.

I have perfect manners.

I dance with princes

and make sure that everyone
in my kingdom is happy.

Everything is just the way I like it.

Until . . .

"Pumpkin?"

"Please call me by my real name!"

"I am . . .

Finally.

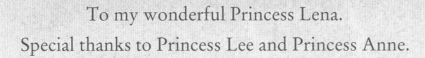

To my wonderful Princess Lena.

Special thanks to Princess Lee and Princess Anne.

Copyright © 2008 by Karen Katz. All rights reserved.
Published in the United States by Schwartz & Wade Books,
an imprint of Random House Children's Books,
a division of Random House, Inc., New York.
SCHWARTZ & WADE BOOKS and colophon are trademarks of
Random House, Inc.
www.randomhouse.com/kids
Educators and librarians, for a variety of teaching tools,
visit us at www.randomhouse.com/teachers
Library of Congress Cataloging-in-Publication Data
Katz, Karen.
Princess Baby / Karen Katz. — 1st ed. p. cm.
Summary: A little girl does not like any of the nicknames her parents
have for her—she wants to be called by her "real" name, Princess Baby.
ISBN: 978-0-375-84119-4 (trade) —
ISBN: 978-0-375-94119-1 (lib. bdg.)
[1. Nicknames—Fiction. 2. Princesses—Fiction.] I. Title.
PZ7.K15745Pr 2008   [E]—dc22   2007001913
The text of this book is set in Stempel Garamond.
The illustrations are rendered in mixed media.
PRINTED IN CHINA
7 9 10 8 6
First Edition